Wilfred:
the worm who would not
Wriggle

by Andrew Bickerton

illustrated by Sally Bishop

Grosvenor House
Publishing Limited

This book is published by
Grosvenor House Publishing Ltd
Link House
140 The Broadway, Tolworth, Surrey, KT6 7HT.
www.grosvenorhousepublishing.co.uk

A CIP record for this book
is available from the British Library

This book is a work of fiction. Any resemblance to
people or events, past or present, is purely coincidental.

ISBN: 978-1-83975-566-8

WILFRED, the worm who would not wriggle.

Cows can't wriggle.

Dogs can't wriggle.

Whales can't wriggle.

Ducks can waddle but they can't wriggle.

Children can giggle and jiggle and sometimes wriggle.

But worms always wriggle. Of course they wriggle.

Pick one up and watch it wriggle.

All worms wriggle.

All except for Wilfred.

He just would not wriggle…

Which is a bit of a problem if you're a worm!

Wilfred used to be able to wriggle.

He was as good at wriggling as any other worm.

Until that dreadful day…

Wilfred was having a lovely time under some rotting leaves, the perfect place for a worm. Many other worms were busy all around him.

He had just finished munching a nice damp oak tree leaf when suddenly the leaves around him were scattered from side to side.

A blackbird was searching for some food!

The next thing he knew he was being lifted into the air with some leaves.

Blackbirds fly.

Sparrows fly

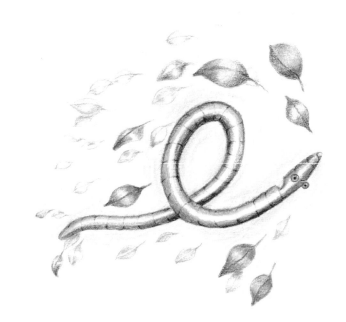

Ducks swim **and** fly.

Eagles soar and fly.

Worms definitely don't fly!

But Wilfred did...

After a few frightening moments flying through the air Wilfred landed with a bump on the ground.

He was stunned and very frightened.

Wilfred was **SCARED STIFF!**

The blackbird snatched worm after worm in his beak and flew off to his nest where the hungry chicks were waiting for their breakfast.

Wilfred didn't want to be breakfast for any birds so he lay **very still**.

After a little while a slippery, slimy slug slithered up to Wilfred.

"What have we here?" sniffed the slug. "A stupid, sleepy worm?"

Wilfred said nothing.

He lay **as stiff as a stick**.

"Won't speak either!"

Wilfred ignored him.

"Stuck up as well!" sneered the slug as it slithered towards some lettuces.

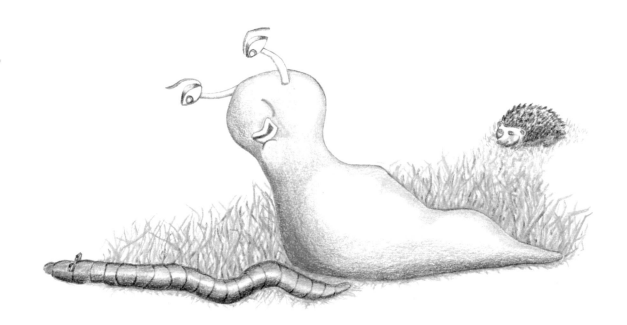

At that moment a prickly hedgehog shuffled and snuffled across the grass.

It saw the slug. "Yum, yum," thought the hedgehog, "a nice snack," and with a **chomp** and a **gulp** it swallowed the slug whole.

"Serves it right!" thought Wilfred,
but then he saw that the hedgehog was coming towards him.

He didn't move.

He didn't breathe.

He was **frozen with fear!**

The snuffling got closer and louder and then…

it grew fainter and fainter as the hedgehog snuffled and shuffled away.

"If I had wriggled," Wilfred thought, "I would have joined that old slug."

"Keeping still saved my life so **keeping still is what I'll do!**"

As Wilfred lay there feeling quite pleased with himself a snail slid past him.

It stopped and stared at Wilfred.

"Come on slowcoach!" it shouted.

Wilfred didn't move.

"Can't even catch a snail!"

Wilfred ignored it.

"Can't catch me! Can't catch me!" laughed the snail as it left Wilfred behind. "Na..na…nanana, can't catch me!"

"**But I can**!" sang a thrush and with a flap and a flutter the thrush flew down. It picked up the startled snail and flew off to find a nice hard stone.

A moment later there was a **crack**

and a **crunch**

and the snail was **lunch**!

"Oh dear," said Wilfred to himself, "it's much too dangerous being out here. I need to hide before some other creature comes along and finds me."

He was just about to begin burrowing into the soft ground when he felt it begin to tremble and shake.

The earth beside him lifted into a big heap.

Wilfred watched as first two large hands followed by a pink nose emerged and then a black, furry body pushed its way to the surface.

It was a mole!

Moles love to eat worms.

In fact, that is just about all they eat!

Wilfred kept **as still as a stone.**

The mole had poor eyesight and it couldn't see Wilfred lying nearby. It wiggled its pink nose, sniffed the clear, fresh air and then…

…sank back into its tunnel leaving behind a large molehill and a **very** relieved Wilfred.

"Now what am I to do?" Wilfred wondered. "The mole will eat me if I go under the soil. Birds or hedgehogs might eat me if I stay here. If I move a hungry creature will see me and eat me. It's hopeless!"

Wilfred felt very sorry for himself. He was full of fear and unable to move.

He was **petrified**!

As night time came a soft rain began to fall and woke Wilfred from his troublesome dreams. The rain brought lots of squirming worms to the surface.

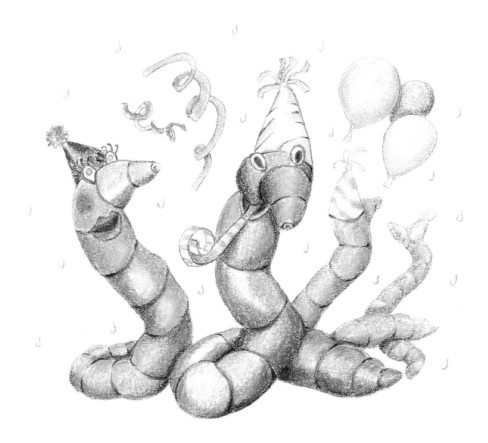

They all seemed very happy. They were having a party!

He would have liked to join the other worms but he remembered all that had happened during that dreadful day so he just lay there,

a sad and lonely worm…

"Hello Wilfred. Why aren't you joining us?" Wilfred looked round and lying next to him was another worm looking exactly like him. It was Wilfreda. Wilfred told her all that had happened that day and why he was so afraid.

"But this is no way for a worm to behave," Wilfreda said. "Worms have to be busy. We have very important work to do.

Without worms rubbish would keep piling higher and higher.

Without worms the soil would be dry and bare.

Without worms many animals would starve.

Without worms many birds would die.

Without our hard work many plants wouldn't grow.

Without worms farmers and gardeners would not be able to grow their crops.

Worms are extremely important"

"But so many worms get eaten by greedy birds and munching hedgehogs and chomping moles!" Wilfred grumbled.

Wilfreda slid her body alongside Wilfred's and whispered soothingly,

"Lots and lots of creatures depend on worms for their food, Wilfred. Without us they would die. We will just have to make sure there are enough worms for everybody. **The more worms the better!"**

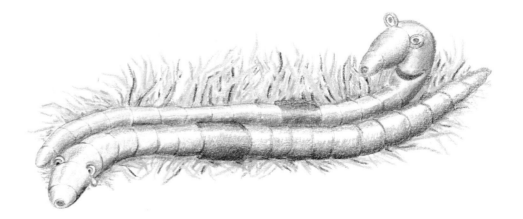

"Follow me," she called as she wriggled over the grass.

"Where are you going?" asked Wilfred.

"I'm going to lay my eggs," she replied. "Come on."

Wilfred began to feel that being a worm was not so bad after all.

"Wait for me," he called. " I think I have some eggs to lay as well. **The more worms the better!"**

And with that Wilfred wriggled happily after her to find a nice soft spot to lay his own eggs.

THE END

THE WONDERFUL WORLD OF WORMS

- There are over twenty different types of worms in Britain

- Earthworms are food for lots of different creatures including: garden birds, gulls, owls, hedgehogs, moles, badgers and frogs

- Worms eat dead leaves and other plant material and recycle it to enrich the soil for plants to grow

- Earthworms burrow in the earth and make the soil able to breath and absorb water

- Without earthworms we would not be able to grow most of the food we eat

- Each earthworm is hermaphrodite; it is both male and female! This means there are twice as many eggs after they mate

Some activities to do

- Search for worms under leaves, logs, and stones. How many different types can you find?

- Watch blackbirds, robins and other birds looking for worms in your garden

- Dig some holes in different parts of your garden and compare the number and type of worms you find. Note which part has the most worms.

- Make a compost pile of leaves and grass cuttings. Worms will love it.

- Look for worm casts on your lawn. They are small heaps of soil that worms leave behind.

- Make a solution of 2 tablespoons of mustard powder in a litre of water and sprinkle it over a square meter of your lawn. Count how many worms come to the surface. **The more worms the better!**

THE WEIRD WORLD OF WORMS!

- There are over 6,000 different types of earthworms in the world.

- Worms do not have any bones.

- Worms do not have any ears, nose or eyes.

- Worms can detect light and prefer darkness.

- Worms have a mouth but it is only used for eating.

- Worms breathe through their skin.

- A worm has 5 hearts.

- Worms have tiny stones and sand in their stomachs to grind up their food.

- Earthworms have many segments between their two ends.

- Each segment has tiny bristles which helps a worm to move and cling to things.

- All earthworms have a complete set of male and female organs inside so there are no boy or girl worms.

MAKING A WORMERY.

A wormery is a special place where worms can grow, make compost and produce more worms. This compost is known as "Gardener's Gold" because it very rich and boosts plant growth. Wormeries can be bought and are available on line but are quite expensive. Making your own wormery is much cheaper and more fun. Below are easy to follow instructions for making your own wormery. Instructions can also be found on YouTube.

1. Find a suitable plastic container about the size of a bucket with a lid.

2. Puncture small holes in the lid and sides.

3. Line the bottom with gravel and small stones for drainage and add shredded damp newspaper for bedding. Then fill up to 2/3 with soil and compost.

4. Collect some worms. Red worms are best. Search under leaves, stones as well as in the earth.

5. Place the worms on the surface of your wormery and close the lid.

6. After a couple of days check your wormery. The worms should have buried into the soil.

7. Keep in a cool shaded place. Add a few raw vegetable scraps once a week.

8. Keep the soil moist but not too soggy. Your compost should be ready after 3-4 weeks.

ABOUT THE AUTHOR

Andrew Bickerton, a retired English teacher, lives in a village in Norfolk. He has written and directed numerous amateur dramatic productions and has published two other children's books highlighting the importance of wildlife and the environment. His first book **"LEAF"** describes the life cycle of a single leaf. **"BUMBLE!"** is a story describing the threats facing bees and other pollinators from chemicals and loss of habitat and **"WILFRED"** continues his writing which aims to teach children about the natural world around us.

ABOUT THE ILLUSTRATOR

Sally Bishop also lives in a Norfolk village, is an artist and designer who loves drawing for her grandchildren. This is her first collaboration with the author. She is keen on the environment, natural habitats and flora and fauna.

CPSIA information can be obtained
at www.ICGtesting.com
Printed in the USA
LVRC100445131021
700312LV00003B/86